DASHAVTAR
THE TEN DIVINE FORMS OF VISHNU

An imprint of Om Books International

Om
KIDZ | Om **Books International**

Reprinted in 2021

Corporate & Editorial Office
A-12, Sector 64, Noida 201 301
Uttar Pradesh, India
Phone: +91 120 477 4100
Email: editorial@ombooks.com
Website: www.ombooksinternational.com

Sales Office
107, Ansari Road, Darya Ganj
New Delhi 110 002, India
Phone: +91 11 4000 9000
Email: sales@ombooks.com

© Om Books International 2008

ISBN: 978-81-87108-39-9

Printed in India

10 9 8 7 6

Contents

Matsya - The Fish
The First Avatar

Once while Lord Brahma was asleep, unknown to him, the Vedas, the holy scriptures, slipped out of his hands. Unfortunately for Brahma, the demon–Hayagriva–was passing by at that time. "These are the Vedas that I have always wanted!" thought Hayagriva. He picked up the Vedas in his mouth and slipped away.

However, Lord Vishnu had seen what Hayagriva had done. "I hardly have any time to lose. Soon it will be time for this age to end and another age to begin," thought Vishnu and looked around. He could see Sage

Satyavrata on Earth offering his daily prayers by taking some water in the hand standing in the river.

Lord Vishnu decided to take the form of a fish. So, the next time the sage bent down to pick up some

water in his hand, he saw a tiny fish in his palms. "I will drop this little one before it dies," he thought, and was about to put it back into the water, when the fish spoke. "The bigger creatures in the river will eat me up. Please take me home with you."

Satyavrata was surprised, but decided to take it home by putting it in his kamandal, a small water pot

held by sages. By the time he got home, the fish had already become bigger. So he put it in a big jar. But the fish grew bigger within hours. Then he decided to take it back to a lake. But the fish kept growing. The sage kept leading the fish to different lakes and rivers; however, it would outgrow the water body within hours.

Finally, it dawned on the sage that this fish was no ordinary one. "You can only be Lord Narayana, another name for Lord Vishnu," said Satyavrata.

"Seven days from now, the waters of all the lakes and seas will swell and submerge the land. You will, however, be saved. Bring the Saptarishis, the seven holy sages, a few chosen animals and birds and Vasuki, the King of Serpents, along with you and board the boat I send," said Lord Narayana.

Then the fish swam to the depths of the ocean to find Hayagriva hiding there, waiting to go on to the next age. With one fatal blow, Matsya, the huge fish killed Hayagriva and took back the Vedas he was hiding.

Seven days later, when the waters swelled, the sages saw a boat sailing towards them. They boarded the boat. A few miles into the water, they found the gigantic fish swimming towards them. It now had a horn on its head. "Tie Vasuki to my horn and I will

take you to the next age," said the fish, and took the boat to safety. Thus ended the Matsya avatar, with all the living beings in the boat moving on to the next age.

Kurma - The Tortoise

The Second Avatar

Sage Durvasa gifted a fragrant garland to Indra, the King of Gods. Indra put the garland on his white elephant, Airavat's head. Sage Durvasa, known for his anger, cursed Indra, "May you and the gods in the heaven become weak and lifeless!"

With that, the demons grew in power day by day. The gods were scared that they could not fight back with the same power they once had. So they decided to seek Lord Vishnu's help. "Churn the ocean to find

the nectar of immortality, which will restore your strength," said Lord Vishnu. "But who will help us in this task?" asked Indra. "The demons," replied Vishnu. "All the three worlds will be destroyed if they drink

the nectar," said Indra. "I promise you that not a drop will be finally given to them," replied Vishnu comforting the gods.

So Indra went to meet Bali, the King of the demons. "We will help you in this task if we also get a share of the nectar," said Bali and made peace with the gods.

They uprooted Mount Mandara to churn the ocean. Lord Vishnu asked Vasuki to become the rope. Thus

began the churning. Before the gods or demons could realise, the mountain slipped from the centre and started getting submerged, as there was nothing to support it at the bottom.

Lord Vishnu took the form of Kurma to save the mountain from going to the depths of the ocean. He held the mountain on his back and helped the gods and demons churn the ocean in their quest for the nectar.

Varaha - The Boar

The Third Avatar

Lord Brahma was busy creating a new age. When Bhoomidevi, Mother Earth, got tossed around in the waves of the ocean and sank into the ocean bed. Brahma was puzzled, as he had no place for the living beings, he was creating, to live in. As he thought hard, he felt a strange being come out from his nostril. It looked like a small boar.

"What is this strange creature coming out of my nostril?", he thought. "Oh! It is Lord Vishnu, in his new avatar of Varaha."

The boar grew in size rapidly and soon was the size of an elephant. It jumped into the ocean and lifted Bhoomidevi on its nose. It then started swimming to the surface.

However, at another end, Hiranyaksha the demon had visited the heaven. "Why don't the gods fight me anymore?" he asked Indra. Without waiting for an answer he went to Varuna, the Lord of Oceans, and challenged him to a fight. "We are too weak for you.

Why don't you fight Lord Vishnu?" asked Varuna. "Where is he?" asked Hiranyaksha. "In the water, in the form of a boar," replied Sage Narada who was passing by.

"Why is he hiding there?" asked Hiranyaksha and jumped into the water. "Fight me you coward!" he shouted at Vishnu in the form of Varaha. But Varaha did not answer and kept swimming back to the surface.

Once Vishnu had placed Bhoomidevi back to where she belonged, he turned back to fight Hiranyaksha. The demon tried to use his mace, but Varaha pulled it from him. Then the boar hit the demon with one of its legs and killed him. Thus ended Varaha avatar, with evil being destroyed once again.

Narasimha - The Man and Lion

The Fourth Avatar

Hiranyaksha's death had deeply hurt Hiranyakashipu, his younger brother. "I will perform a severe penance and kill the gods," thought the demon and retired to the forest. Lord Indra learnt of this and declared war on the demons. Many demons were killed and many were captured by the gods and were taken back to the heaven.

Hiranyakashipu's wife was pregnant and was being taken to the heaven with other prisoners, when Sage Narada saw her. "Leave her in my care, Indra," said Narada, and took her to his humble

house. There he recited all the holy scriptures and the unborn one heard all of it from his mother's womb.

Lord Brahma finally appeared before Hiranyakashipu and asked him to choose a boon. "I seek immortality," said the demon. "That I cannot give," said Brahma. "In that case, I should not be killed by a human or an animal; not with any weapon; not in the morning or night; neither indoors nor outdoors; not on earth nor in the sky," said Hiranyakashipu, thinking he had asked for a boon, which would ensure that he would never die. Brahma granted him the boon and the demon returned to his evil ways. The gods were driven out of their homes and the demons ruled.

Hiranyakashipu's son, Prahlad, was sent to study at an ashram. But Prahlad, was a devotee of Lord Vishnu as he had heard only his praises while he was in the womb of his mother.

His father had declared himself to be god, but Prahlad refused to accept him as god. "You will be killed, if you don't accept me as god, Prahlad," thundered Hiranyakashipu.

But Prahlad did not change his stand. So he was attacked by elephants, thrown into a pit of dangerous serpents, made to sit in a pyre with his aunt Holika to be burnt alive. But he survived all these dangers, chanting the name of Lord Vishnu.

"If your Vishnu is so powerful, ask him to fight me," said Hiranyakashipu. "Where is he?" asked the demon. "He is everywhere," replied Prahlad. "Is he in this pillar?" asked Hiranyakashipu.

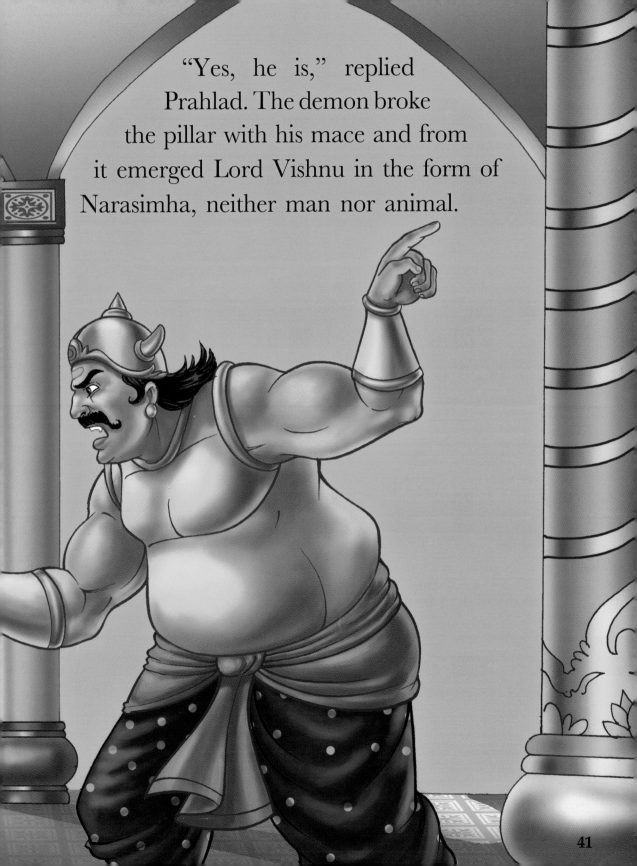

"Yes, he is," replied Prahlad. The demon broke the pillar with his mace and from it emerged Lord Vishnu in the form of Narasimha, neither man nor animal.

He had the face of a lion and the body of a man. He carried the demon to the threshold of the palace, neither inside nor outside; put him on his lap, neither on earth nor in the sky and tore his stomach with his claws, no weapon, at twilight, neither morning nor night.

Narasimha restored peace and righteousness to the three worlds. He crowned Prahlad as the King of the Demons.

Vamana - The Midget

The Fifth Avatar

Many generations later, Bali, the grandson of Prahlad, became the King of the demons, and won over the rule of the three worlds from the gods. Aditi, the mother of the gods, performed a vow for twelve long days to please Lord Vishnu. "Help my sons get back

the power they have lost," she pleaded with the Lord when he appeared in front of her.

Lord Vishnu took the form of a midget-sized man and went to meet Bali, who was performing a holy sacrifice. "I have come for alms," said Vishnu in the

form of Vamana. "You have come at the right time. Ask for what you desire," said Bali. "I need only three spaces of land measuring three steps of mine," said Vamana. "Granted!" replied Bali, only to be warned

by his teacher, Shukracharya that Vamana was Vishnu in disguise.

"Once I have granted a boon, I will not take it back, whoever it is," said Bali and looked at Vamana. His wife washed Vamana's feet, only to find him growing. He grew as high as the space between the earth and the sky. With one step of his, he covered the entire earth and the pataal, what lies below the earth. With the second he covered the heaven.

"I have covered all that you own. But I still have one more step left. What do I do?" asked Vamana. "You have my head," replied Bali and bowed before him.

Vamana gently pushed Bali down. "You have earned your place in my heart and the heaven by fulfilling your word, despite knowing who I am," said Vamana before disappearing.

Parashurama

The Sixth Avatar

Kartavirya Arjuna, was the ruler of a sect called the Haihayas. He had a thousand hands. Arjuna had prayed to Lord Dattatreya and got boons, which made him all-powerful. He tortured those on earth and the heaven.

Lord Vishnu took the form of Parashurama and was born as the youngest son of Sage Jamadagni and Renuka. From his childhood, he knew a lot about weapons and carried the axe at all times as his weapon. "My Parashurama is a born warrior," thought Jamadagni looking at his son.

As days passed, Parashurama grew up to be a fine young man. One day, Arjuna was passing by Parashurama's house. Sage Jamadagni invited him and his men for lunch. "We are too many of us,"

said Arjuna. "When I have Kamadhenu, why should I worry?" said the sage and looked at the holy cow. Just as the sage had said, Kamadhenu gave unlimited food to everyone.

"If the holy cow can give so much, why can't she be mine?" thought Arjuna and walked away from the ashram. His soldiers returned to the sage's ashram and

took away Kamadhenu and her calf forcefully. When Parashurama came to know about this, he was furious and stormed to Arjuna's palace. Arjuna sent many warriors to defeat him, but all of them fell dead with Parashurama's fatal blows.

Finally, it was Arjuna's turn. Parashurama cut off his thousand hands and killed him, restoring peace on land!

Rama - The Seventh Avatar

Ravana had become the King of the Demons. Lord Vishnu took the form of Rama, the eldest son of King Dasharatha of Ayodhya. King Dasharatha had three wives—Kaushalya, Kaikeyi and Sumitra—and four sons—Rama, Bharata, Lakshmana and Shatrughna.

Rama killed many evil demons in his childhood. He married Sita, the daughter of King Janak. In order to please mother Kaikeyi, he had to retire to the forest for fourteen years with Sita and his brother Lakshmana. In the forest, Soorpanakha, the sister of Ravana, insisted on marrying Rama. But Lakshmana insulted her by cutting off

her nose. This angered Ravana. He sent a demon in the form of a golden deer and diverted Rama's attention towards getting the deer for his wife. Then he disguised himself as a sage and kidnapped Sita, when she came to give him alms.

But Rama, with the help of the monkeys and his biggest devotee,

Hanuman, built a bridge over the seas to Lanka and waged a war against Ravana and his evil forces. Rama killed Ravana and crowned his brother Vibhishana as the King of the demons, and returned to Ayodhya.

Krishna

The Eighth Avatar

Lord Vishnu was born as the eighth child of Devaki and Vasudeva, whom the evil Kansa had imprisoned. He was taken to safety by Vasudeva, who handed him over to Nand, at Gokul. Krishna was raised in Gokul, but was known for killing all the demons sent by Kansa.

From Putana—who tried to poison him in his childhood by feeding him poison—to Trinavarta—the demon who came in the form of a whirlwind—to Aghasura— who came in the form of serpent and tried to swallow Krishna—and Dhenukasura—who appeared as a donkey—every demon was killed by Krishna!

Krishna and Balarama, Krishna's elder brother, finally reached Mathura, the capital of Kansa and challenged him to a duel. There, Krishna killed Kansa with his bare hands. Krishna grew to be the darling of all. He had sixteen thousand wives and was the

closest friend of the Pandavas. He helped them win back their kingdom, which was taken away by Duryodhana. In the war, known as the famous Mahabharata, Krishna recited the *Bhagavad Gita* to Arjuna.

Krishna's life ended on earth, when a hunter shot an arrow at his foot, when he was sitting under a tree. The hunter mistook the foot showing from behind a bush as the mouth of a deer.

Buddha
The Ninth Avatar

King Shuddhodhana and Queen Mayadevi of Kapilavastu were blessed with a son, whom they named Siddhartha. The boy grew up to be a fine prince and was married to Yashodhara. Soon,

they were blessed with a son. But Siddhartha met his father with a desire one day. "I want to go out and see the world," he said. "I will give you my chariot,"

said Shuddhodhana. Every time Siddhartha rode out of the palace, he saw the truths of life, he had never known—old age, illness and death.

But one day, he saw a monk meditating. "Why is his face so calm?" he asked his charioteer. "He has decided to devote his life in trying to find real happiness," replied the charioteer. That night, Siddhartha made up his mind to give up the worldly pleasures and retire to the forests. He sat under a Bodhi tree for days and gained enlightenment as Buddha—the learned one.

Kalki - The Tenth Avatar

This is the only form of Lord Vishnu that remains to be taken. The holy books believe that when evil on the Earth goes beyond its limits, Lord Vishnu will take the form of a soldier on a horse and bring back peace. Known as the yet-to-be taken Kalki avatar, it will be the end of the ten forms of Vishnu, and the beginning of a new era...

OTHER TITLES IN THIS SERIES

 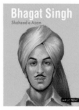 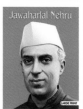 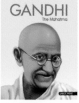   

 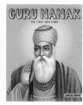  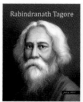 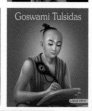 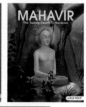 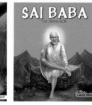